ONE GORILLA

JOY DEY

NIKKI JOHNSON

SWAK
PUBLISHING™
DULUTH, MINNESOTA

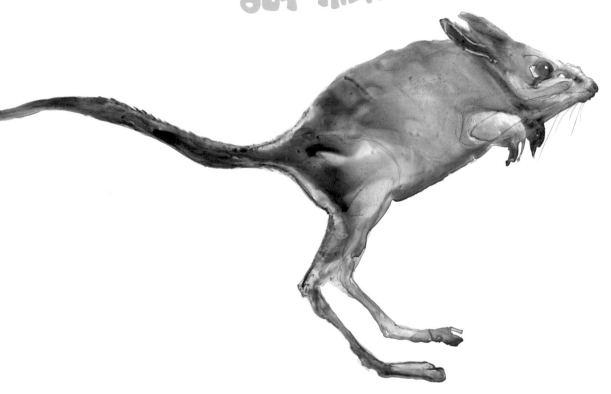

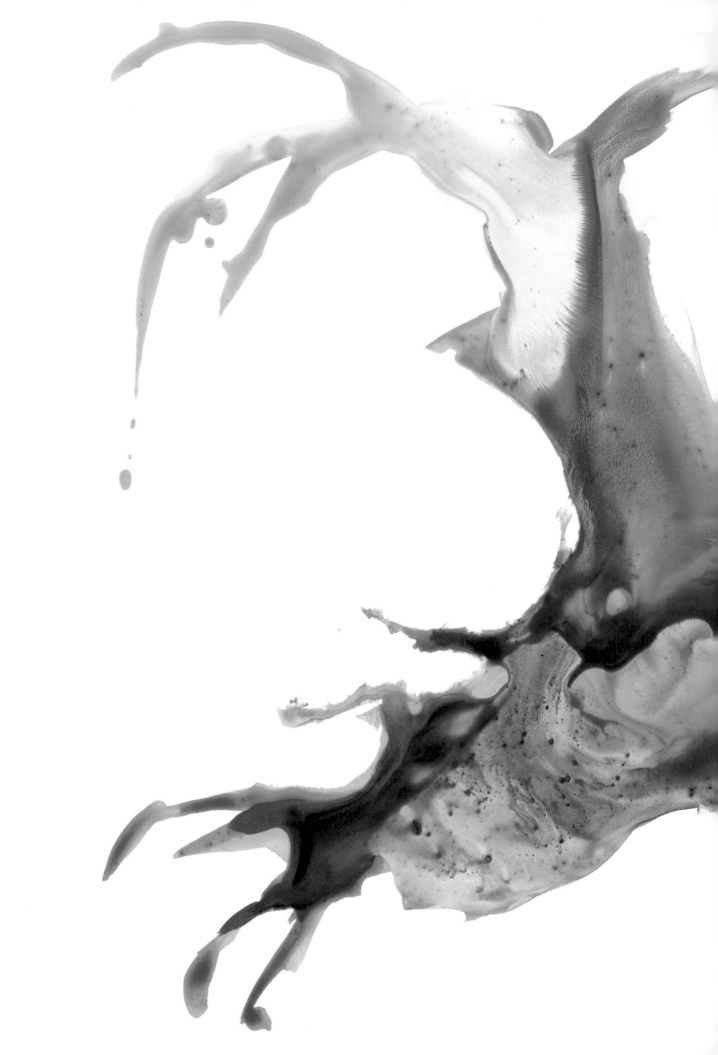

Prowling, savage, tooth and claw,

THE JUNGLE

crouches and glares.

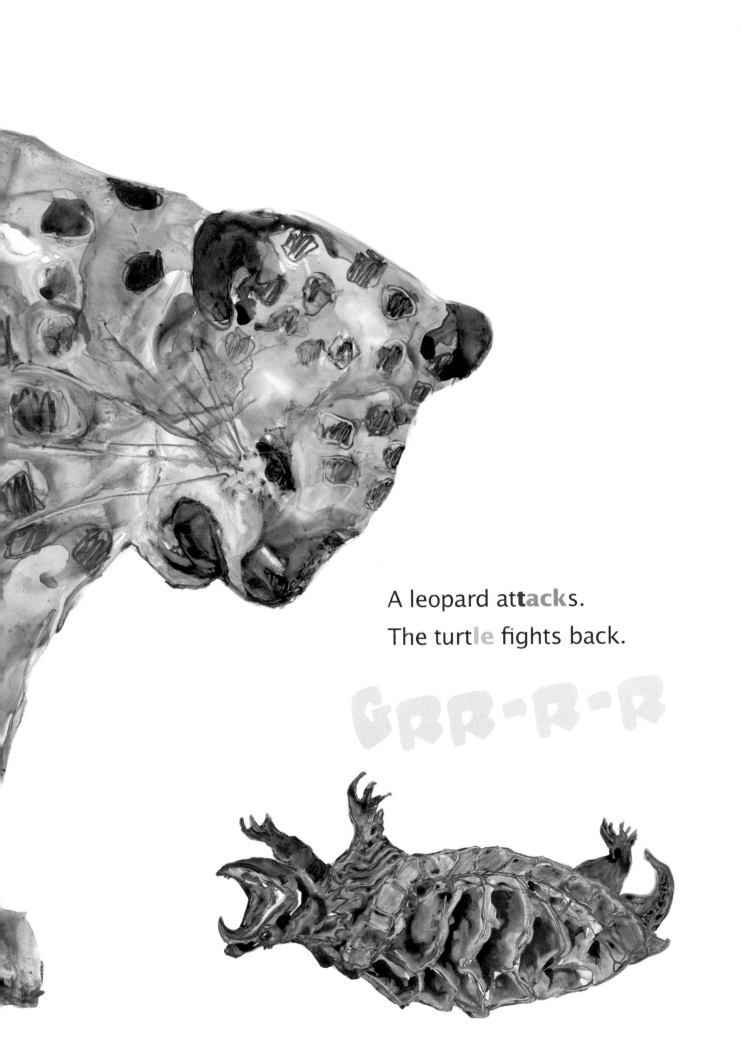

A leopard at**tack**s.

The turt**le** fights back.

GRR-R-R

Wicked wo**m**bats trip giraff**e**s
and twist the lemur's tail.

OW-W-W-W

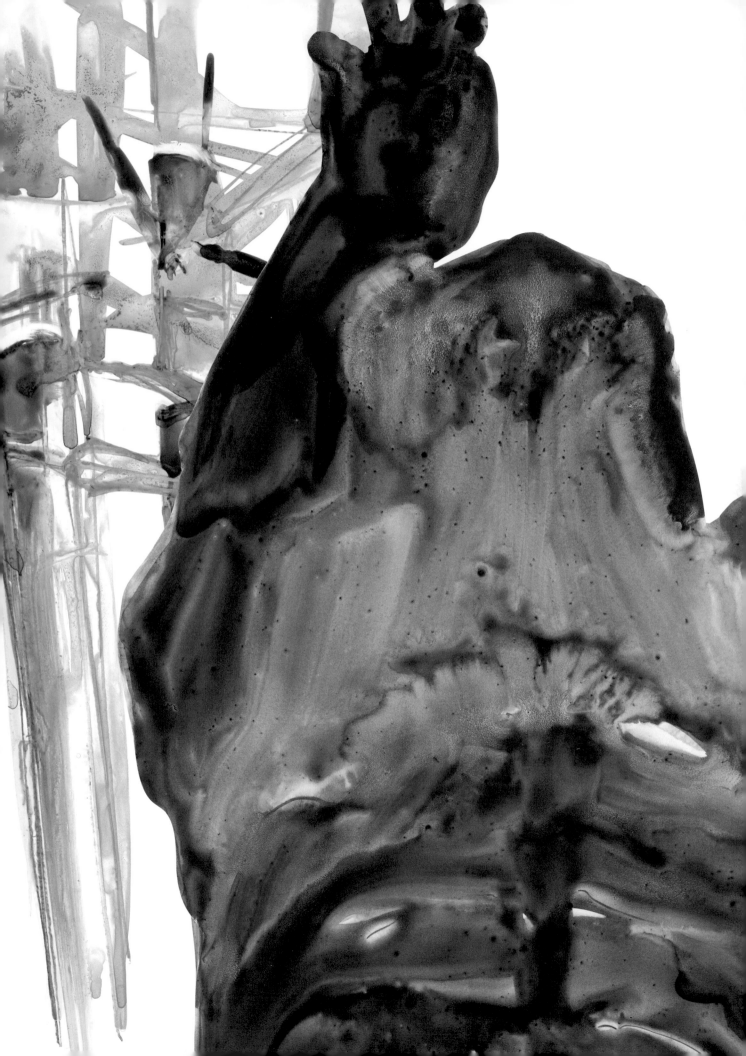

A **w**ild-eyed ape
thumps and s**h**oves,
kicking **a**nthills
and kno**ck**ing down trees.

RA-A-A-R

IT'S A JUNGLE OUT THERE!

. . . a free-for-all,
a nightmare of
rotten behavior.
It's a
booga-looga
cowabunga
jungle.

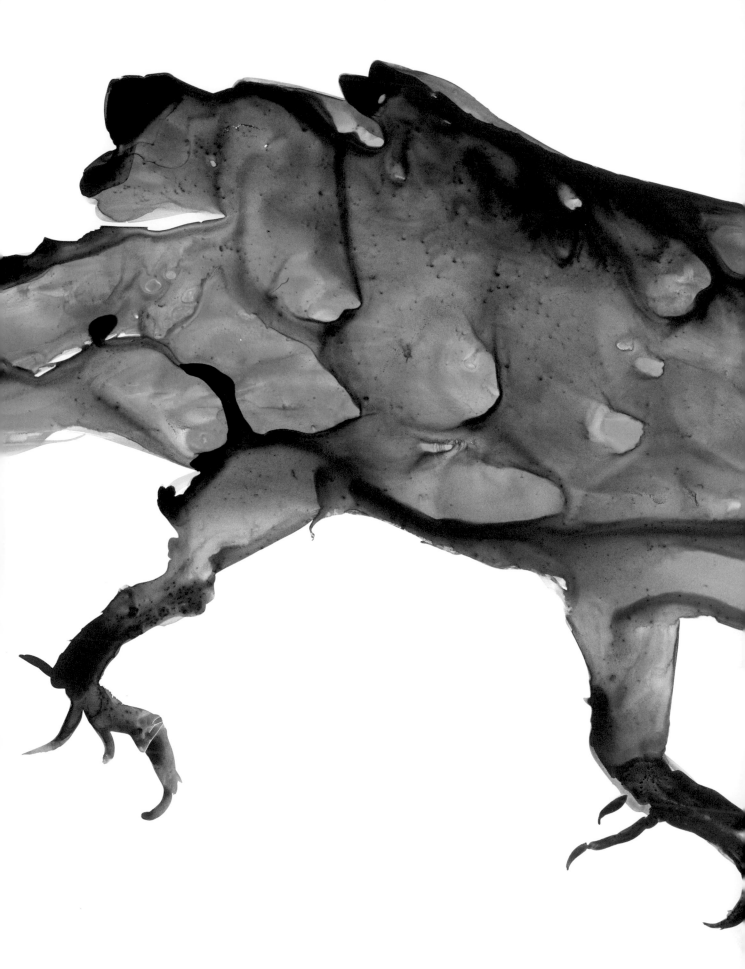

Fabulous par**rot**s flash **t**heir claws,
shri**e**king at rats and bats a**n**d frogs.

BRA-A-AWCK

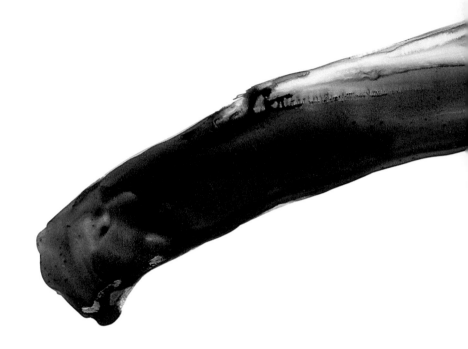

Even the anteater's itching to fight.
Keep your paws off his dirt and his mites.

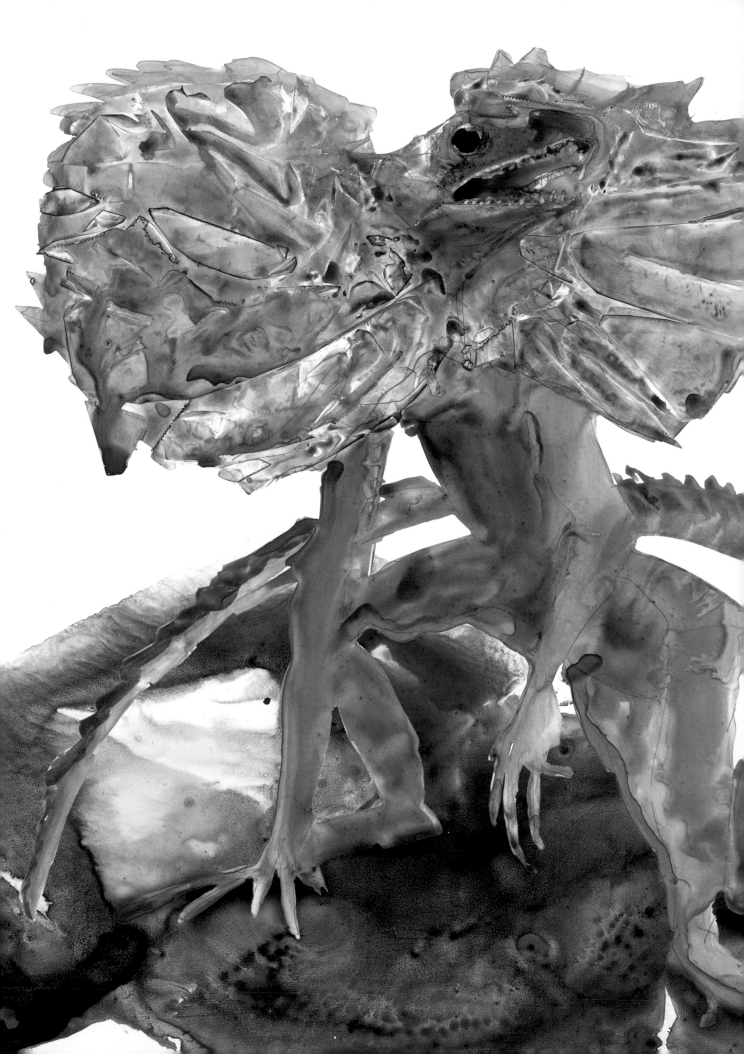

A **c**ranky lizard sl**eep**s on a rock,
her head full of geckos and toads.
Beastl**y** screams shatter her dreams.

SSS-S-S-S

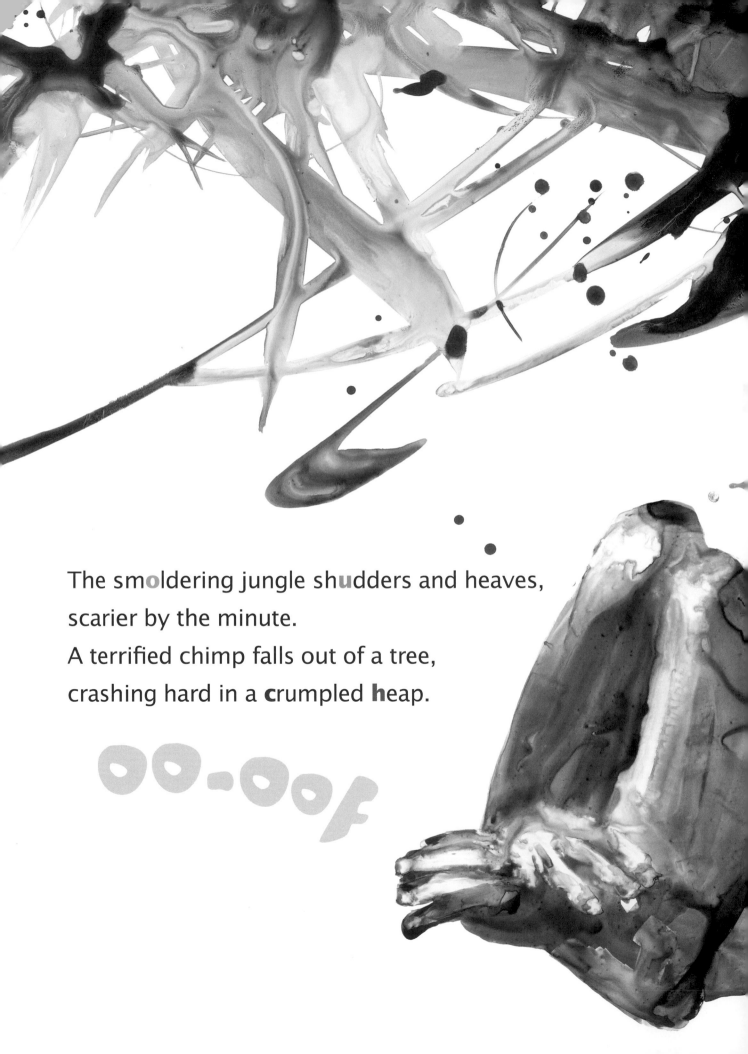

The smoldering jungle shudders and heaves,
scarier by the minute.
A terrified chimp falls out of a tree,
crashing hard in a crumpled heap.

OO-OOF

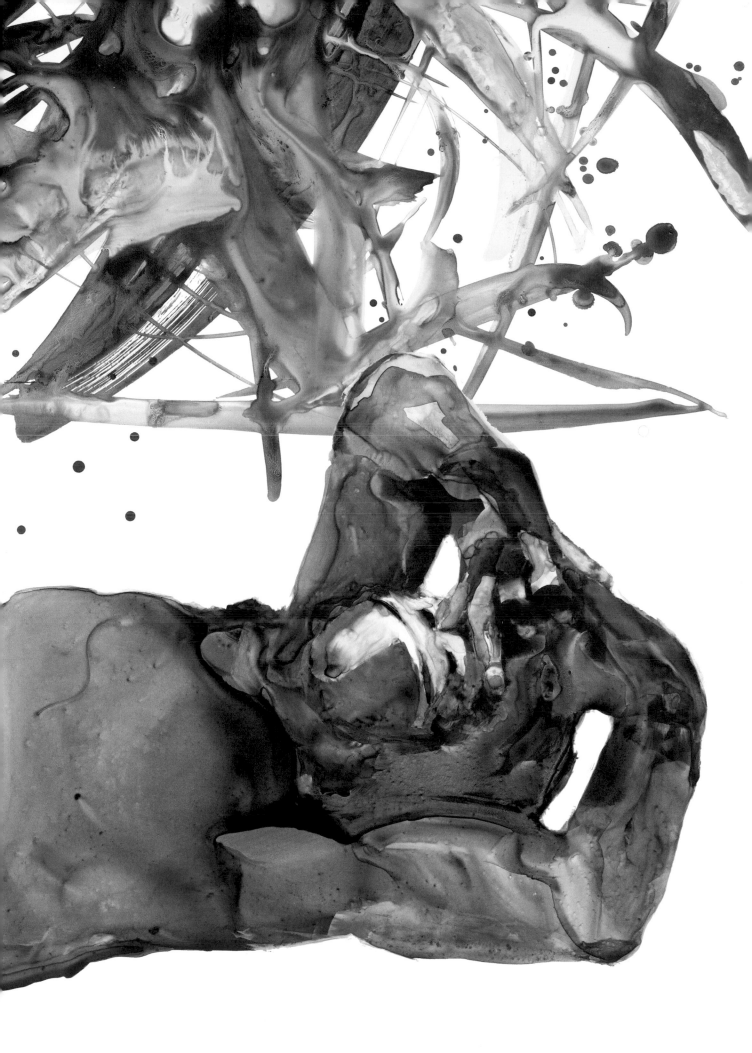

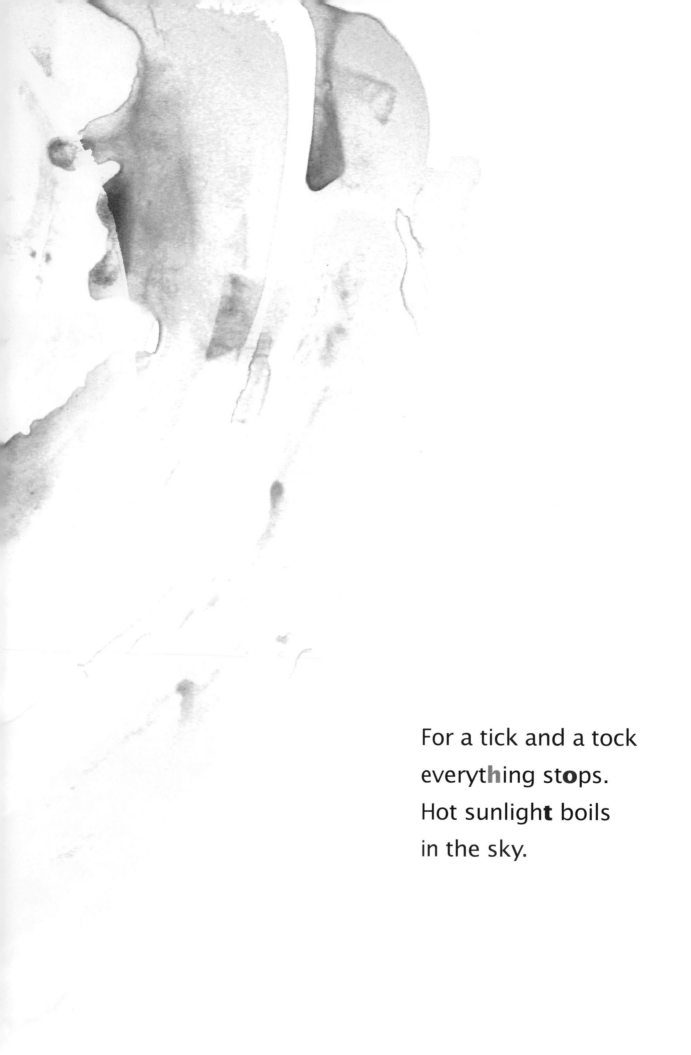

For a tick and a tock
everything stops.
Hot sunlight boils
in the sky.

Then one little giggle
breaks the spell.

Hee-hee-hee.

And . . .

THE WHOLE
WACKY
JUNGLE
CRACKS
UP!

Sniggering baboons
jump up and down.
Magpies cackle
and snort.

Cheetahs and peacocks,
hyenas and storks
laugh so hard it hurts.

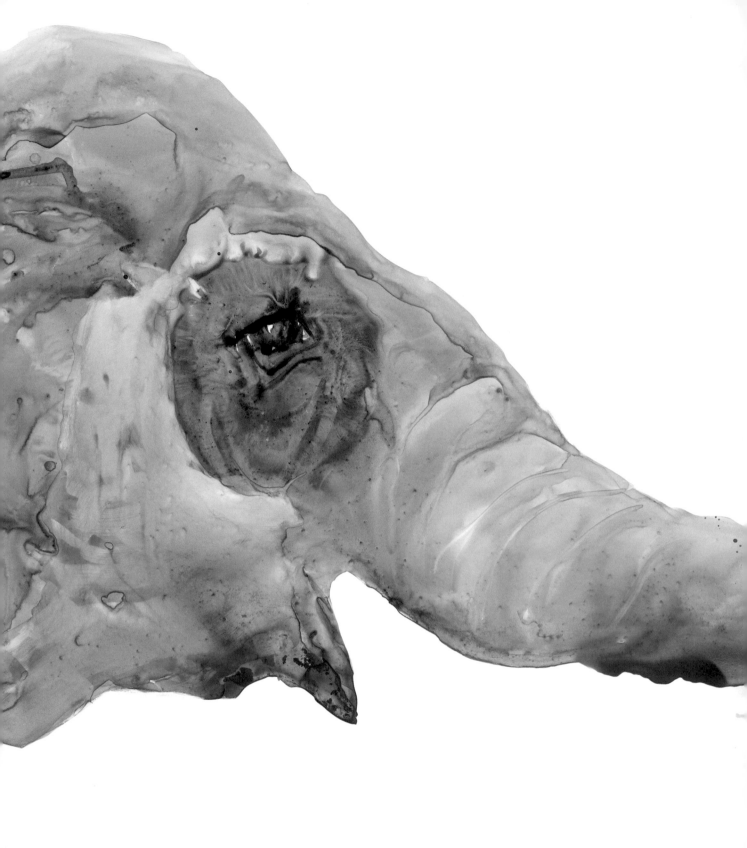

The elephants wheeze and stomp around.
They point and **s**nicker and smirk.

Except for **o**ne.
He knows that hurt.
His hea**rt** goes out to the chimp.

With a slobbe**ry** kiss and a rubbery hug
he helps her get back up.

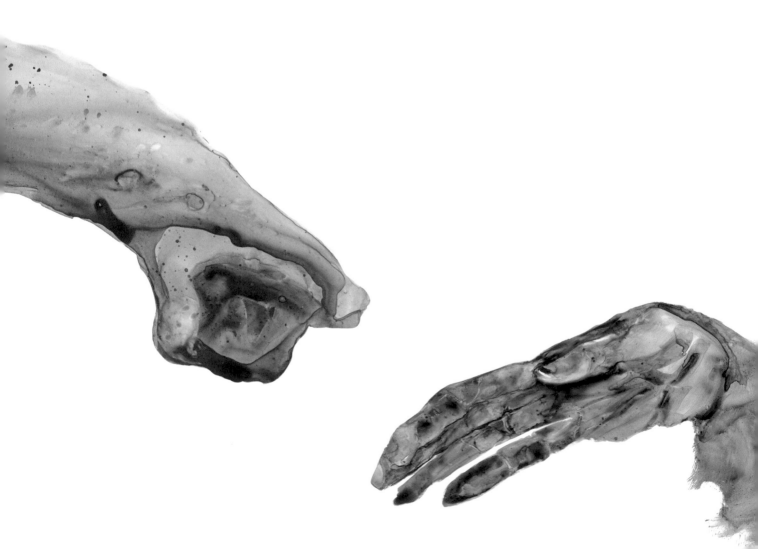

Skaree-e-ek! Ka-thunk!
The laughter stops.
The jungle falls silent.

It's thinking.

It's a hushed and dreamy,
lush and steamy,

SOMETHING'S
DIFFERENT
JUNGLE

The chimp is okay.
She looks around,
not too sure what just happened.

She blinks and shivers
and skitters away.

Just a skip and a scamper down the road,
the chimp spots a sweaty rhino.

She always beans him with a rock.
She's done it a million times.
But today, for some strange reason, she stops . . .

. . . and splashes cool water instead!

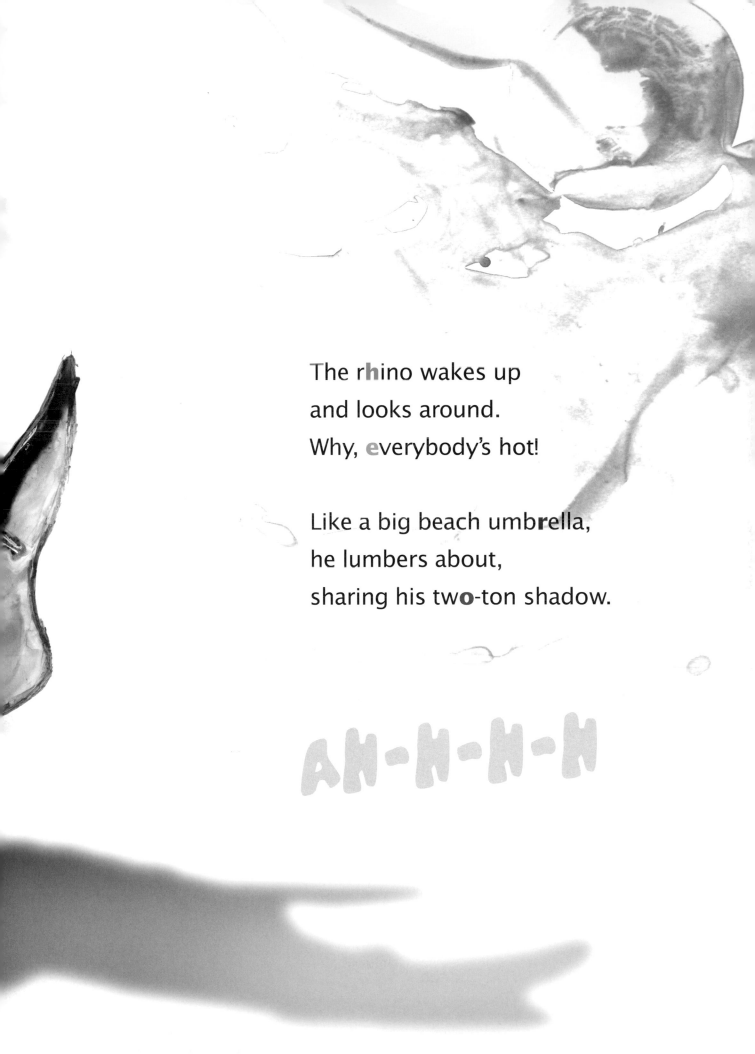

The **r**hino wakes up
and looks around.
Why, **e**verybody's hot!

Like a big beach umb**r**ella,
he lumbers about,
sharing his tw**o**-ton shadow.

AH-H-H-H

The snake gets a share of the rhino shade,
so she's in a good mood, hangin' loose.
She guards a snoozing flying fox.

ZZZ-Z-Z-Z

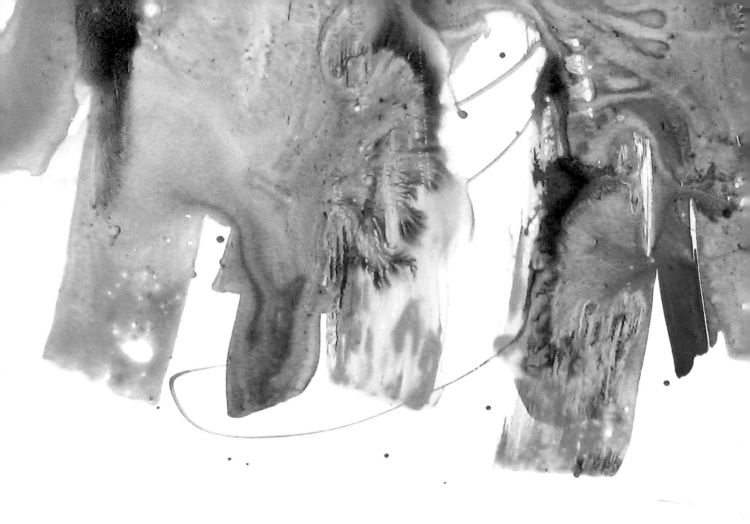

And now—get this!—the flying fox
is thinking of sharing his mango!

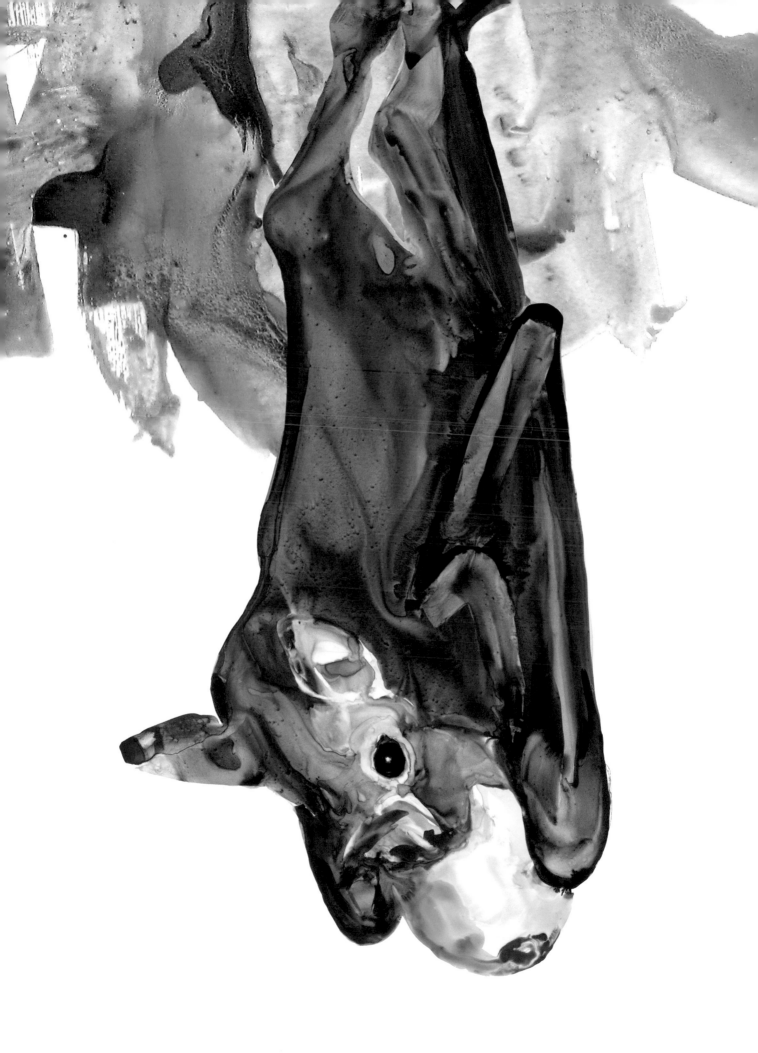

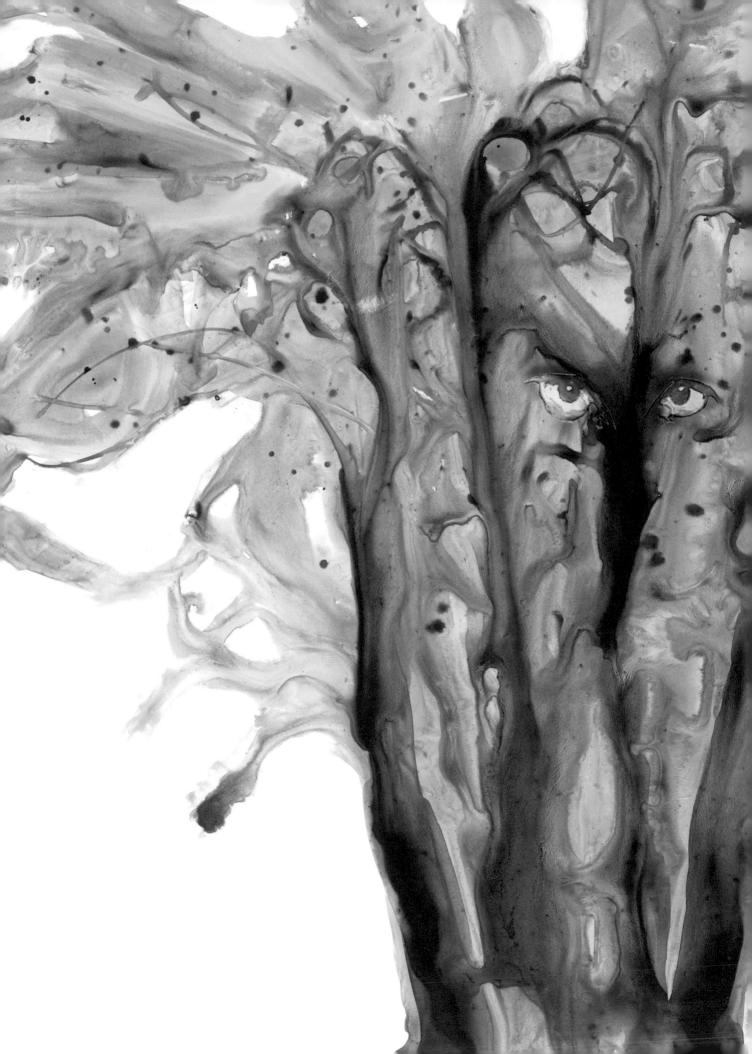

It's a little bit brighter

JUNGLE

out there.

Not so much growling
and hissing.

But have things really **ch**anged?
Let's just w**a**tch.

ONE GORILLA COULD ROCK THE WORLD!

Cross your fi**n**gers
and hold your br**e**ath...

He **c**ould spin t**h**e turtle.
He c**o**uld tickle her silly.
He c**o**uld stick her up in a tree.

But what if he turn**s** her right sid**e** up?

HOLY COCONUTS!

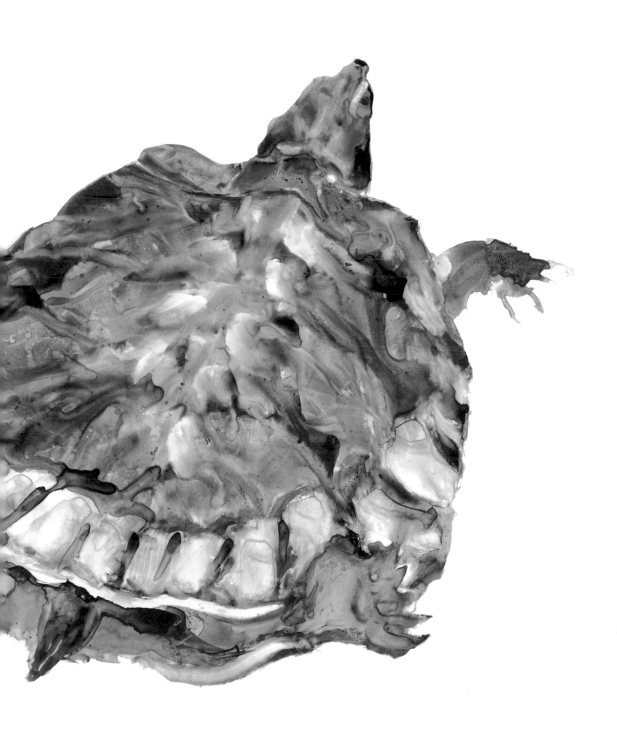

For Mark, Cy and Nancy, Anna and James, Rosy and Ben, Alex, Zach, Brody.
For Tom, Mom and Dad, Burl, Sydney, Alex, Connie, Aunt Parry, Jim and Elaine.
And for all of you who light up the jungle every single day.

Special thanks to . . .
Sister Sharon Waldoch; Linda Hanson, Ann Hoak, and Jill Lyman
at Barnes and Noble; Lynn Pepin; Anita Zaeger; Bill Gates;
Carlene Sippola; Don and Nancy Tubesing; Holy Rosary Elementary;
Steven "Tigg" Tiggeman at CPL Imaging; and
Dennis Anderson, WDIO, "Goodnight and be kind."

And to schools and educators everywhere,
thank you for your daily good deeds
in promoting reading and caring behavior
in our kids.

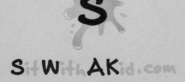

SitWithAKid.com

Published by **SWAK Publishing LLC**,
7064 Old Vermilion Trail, Duluth, Minnesota 55803

Library of Congress Control Number 2014935690. Cataloging-in-Publication data available. ISBN 978-0-9853228-2-3.

Printed in Canada by Friesens Corporation.